Book Name: Children of Jannah
Written by: Redha al-Haidari, Misdaq R Syed
Edited by: Misdaq R Syed
Illustrated by: Zahraa Mohammad
Publisher: Al-Buragh for Children`s Culture
Design and technical supervision: Mohammed Alqasemi
Published Year: 2024
ISBN: 9789922704586

30 Stories

Children of Jannah
Little stories for little children

Written by: Redha al-Haidari, Misdaq R Syed
Illustrated by: Zahraa Mohammad

Contents of the book

Who Feeds the Chicks?

In the world, there are so many beautiful things to see, like colorful paintings and amazing artwork. We often admire them and say, "Wow, what a fantastic artist!" But have you ever wondered about the artist behind everything in nature, like the pretty flowers, the fluttering butterflies, the singing birds, the glistening rivers, the trees full of yummy fruits? They all seem to be saying, "Thank you, Creator!"

Once upon a time, there was a man who didn't believe in god. He decided to visit a wise scholar to find answers to his questions. The scholar's son was playing with a chicken egg, and he took the egg from him and said, "Look closely at this egg. It's like a strong fortress! It has a thick, protective shell, and inside that, there's a delicate, thin one. In the center, there's a clear, silver-like liquid, and a golden, liquid sphere. But the magic is that they never mix! When a chicken lays an egg, she keeps it warm for three weeks, and inside, a little chick starts to grow. When it's time, the chick hatches with its beautiful colors. A duck's egg hatches a duckling that can swim in the water. A bird's egg hatches a bird that can soar in the sky. A chicken's egg hatches chicks that run around with their mother. But who is taking care of the chicks inside the eggs? Who taught the birds how to swim and fly?"

The man began to think deeply, and slowly but surely, he began to see the light of faith in his heart.

How do we love you my Lord?

Allah, the Most High, once spoke to His dear prophet, Musa (peace be upon him), and said, "Musa, love Me, and help others love Me too." Musa replied, "My Lord, I love You more than anything in the whole world! But how can I help people love You?" Allah replied, "Musa, remind them of all the wonderful things I've given them. When they remember My gifts, they'll remember Me and love Me."

So, my friends, let's think about the amazing things Allah has given us. Look around you, and you'll see so many special gifts from Him. He made us and gave us life, the gift of intellect, the ability to hear and see. He also made the sun and the moon, sent us rain for the plants, and provided us with tasty fruits and fresh, clean water to drink. All these amazing things are blessings from Allah, our Creator. And here's something really wonderful – He put a lot of love in parents' hearts for their children. That's another of His blessings. When we remember all these gifts, our love for Allah gets stronger, and our faith in Him grows. So, always remember the good things from Allah, and you'll feel His love in your heart.

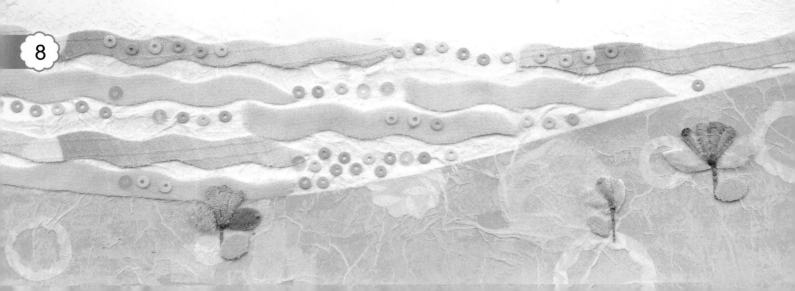

Would you please give me some water?

Once upon a time, in a faraway place, there was a man who didn't have many friends because he didn't believe in God and wasn't very nice to others. One day, he came across a deep well and saw a poor, thirsty dog circling it, extending its tongue helplessly. The dog looked at the man with sad eyes, as if saying, "I'm so thirsty."

The man felt something deep inside his heart. You see, Allah, our Creator, has given humans the gift of kindness and love. Even though the man didn't have a bucket to get water from the well, he had an idea. He took off his shirt, held one of its sleeves, and carefully dipped it into the well. He waited for a moment until the cloth soaked up some water, and then he pulled it up. The dog saw the water dripping from the shirt and eagerly drank from it. The man did this again and again until the dog wasn't thirsty anymore. The dog wagged its tail happily and then went on its way.

When the man went back home, some people continued to turn their faces away from him as they used to, but something amazing happened. Their prophet, a wise and kind person, greeted him warmly. This surprised everyone. The prophet explained, "Allah has told me that He is happy with you and has forgiven your mistakes." The man asked, "But why?" The prophet replied, "It's because you showed kindness to that thirsty dog. Allah loves those who are kind and gentle to His creatures."

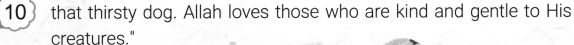

When the man heard this, he decided to change his ways, be kind to others, and follow the right path.

11

❧ More than the love of parents... ❧

Every parent loves their children a lot. They stay awake when their little ones need comfort, and they work hard to provide them with food, clothes, and a happy life. You see, a mother won't sleep until she feeds her baby, and if the baby wakes up in the middle of the night crying, she rushes to make everything better.

But there's a love even greater than this, and it's the love that God has for us. God's love for us is bigger than a parent's love for their child.

Once, the Prophet Muhammad (s) was sitting in the mosque, and one of his friends came with his little child. The friend sat down, hugged his child, gave him sweet kisses, and gently patted his hair. The Prophet asked his friend, "Do you love your son?" His friend answered, "Yes, Messenger of Allah, I love him very much." The Prophet (s) smiled and said, "You know, Allah loves His servants even more than a Father loves his child... because Allah is the Most Merciful of all who show mercy."

So, remember, you are very, very special to God, and His love for you is the most wonderful love of all.

12

Can we be kind to Allah?

Allah, our Most High and Loving Creator, loves His servants who are kind to their fellow humans. When we help someone in need, it's like we're helping Allah Himself, and He rewards us for our kindness And here's a special thing to know: On the Day of Judgment, when we meet Allah, He will talk to us about how we were kind to others.

Allah might say, "Hey, remember that time when I was sick, and you didn't come to visit me?" But we might be confused and say, "You're the Healer, Allah, how could You be sick?" And then Allah will explain, "My servant was sick, and you didn't visit them. If you had visited them, it would be like you visited Me."

Then Allah might say, "Remember when I asked you for water, and you didn't give me any?" We might wonder, "You're the Lord, Allah, you don't need water!" But Allah will say, "My servant asked you for water, and you didn't give it to them. If you had given them water, it would be like you gave Me water."

And finally, Allah might say, "You know when I asked you for food, and you didn't feed me?" We might say, "But You're the Provider, Allah, how can we feed You?" And Allah will say, "My servant asked you for food, and you didn't feed them. If you had fed them, it would be like you fed Me."

So, being kind to others is really special to Allah. When we do good things for others, it's like we're doing them for Allah, and He's pleased with us. So, let's be kind and helpful to those around us, and Allah will be proud of our kindness.

❧ The Old Woman and the Spinning Wheel... ❧

One day, the Prophet Muhammad (s) came across an elderly woman who was diligently working her spinning wheel to create threads. Curious, he asked her, "How do you come to know Allah, old woman?"

The elderly woman paused her spinning wheel by lifting her hand, explaining, "This spinning wheel only stops when I choose to stop it, for it doesn't move on its own. Now, consider this vast universe with its lands, skies, the radiant sun, the gleaming moon, and countless stars. Doesn't it too require someone to set it in motion, to make the sunrise and the moon shine?" The Prophet (a)smiled, recognizing the wisdom in her words.

Indeed, our world is like an incredible spinning wheel. Earth rotates on its axis, giving us day and night, while it orbits the sun, granting us the changing seasons. This movement leads to shifts in temperature and climate, bringing rain, flowing rivers, and fertile fields and orchards that provide us with food.

Yet, amidst the countless celestial bodies in the universe, this spinning wheel of Earth keeps turning tirelessly, never coming to a halt or breaking down. Why is that? What if it stopped suddenly?

The undeniable truth is that behind this universe stands an Almighty Creator who guides it. Without His continuous care and gifts, it would cease to function. It's this realization that leads one to believe in the greatness of Allah, the Creator of all.

❧ The Sound of the Worm in the Sea... ❧

Allah, our Most High and Powerful Creator, sees and hears everything in this amazing world. He can hear the tiniest sounds, like the footsteps of ants and the whispering of leaves in the trees. He can even see the small creatures that live deep in the mysterious depths of the dark seas. And it's not just that; He also takes care of them and makes sure their lives go smoothly.

Once, the Prophet Dawud (a) climbed a tall mountain to pray and talk to Allah. The mountain overlooked the sea.

18

After he had finished his prayers,
the Angel Jibril (a) came with Allah's
permission and took him on a magical journey
deep into the sea. They traveled until they reached
a big rock. Jibril then lifted the rock and showed a tiny
worm underneath it.

Prophet Dawud was told, 'Indeed, Allah, the Almighty, hears
the sounds of the rocks at the bottom of the sea, all of them. Even
the sound of this tiny worm under this rock.'

SubhanAllah, Allah is the truly the most magnificent and
wonderful Creator of all.

19

❧ The Reward of a Visit... ❧

Once, a man left his home to visit his fellow believers, seeking the pleasure of Allah. As he approached his friend's door, something extraordinary happened. Allah, the Most High, sent one of His angels ahead to meet the man. The angel inquired, "What brings you here?"

The man replied, "I have come to visit my dear brother."

The angel continued, "And why have you undertaken this journey?"

The man's eyes sparkled with faith, and he answered, "I'm here solely to seek Allah's pleasure.

The angel shared a wonderful secret, saying, "Know this, Allah has declared, 'Whoever visit their brothers with the intention of seeking My pleasure are akin to visiting Me, I shall reward them with Paradise.'"

The man couldn't believe his ears and thought, "Who are you, my visitor?"

With a warm smile, the angel revealed, "I am one of Allah's cherished messengers, here to bring you joyful tidings. Allah sends His blessings and says, 'I appreciate your visit to Me, and I shall grant you admission to Paradise.'"

With that, the angel disappeared from sight, leaving the man's heart brimming with love and joy.

The Reward without Effort...

Once, there lived a virtuous man who was dedicated to doing good deeds. He helped the poor, regularly visited the mosques for prayer and knowledge, and showed kindness to his neighbors. The angels kept a record of all these noble actions.

One day, the man fell seriously ill and was bedridden, unable to leave his house. He couldn't greet his neighbors, visit the mosque, or help any needy person. He missed his visits to the mosque, offering greetings to his neighbors, and assisting those in need. The angels noticed that his good deeds were no longer being recorded.

Allah, the Most High, then sent an inspiration to them, 'Why are you not writing the deeds of this faithful believer?'

The angels respectfully replied, "We no longer see him at the mosque, and he cannot greet his neighbors due to his illness."

In response, Allah said, "Write down all the good deeds he used to perform when he was in good health, and continue to record them until he recovers from his illness."

23

The Magnificent Kingdom...

Our world is like a majestic banquet, and it's filled with countless guests who eat until they're satisfied and drink until they're content. If you look at the towering mountains, you'll find wild goats happily grazing on the lush grass. In the depths of the oceans, mighty whales gracefully feast on small fish. Fields of green are a paradise for cattle and livestock. In the vast deserts, camels search for their sustenance. And within the heart of dense forests, lions, tigers, and cheetahs are skilled hunters, seeking their prey. Every creature, every bird, every living being participates in this magnificent banquet of life.

Prophet Sulaiman, known for his wisdom, was once the greatest king on Earth. He commanded armies of humans, jinn, and even birds. His feasts were legendary, and even lions joined in the grand meal.

One day, Prophet Sulaiman stood by the seashore, and a massive whale approached him, asking for food. The Prophet agreed and ordered the preparation of numerous gigantic pots. To his astonishment, the whale swiftly devoured them all. He inquired, "Is there anyone in the sea who eats more than you?" The whale responded, "Indeed, there are thousands who eat more than I do."

Sulaiman looked up at the sky and exclaimed, "How wondrous is Your Kingdom, O Lord!" Truly, the Kingdom of God is beyond our wildest imagination.

The Best Knowledge is Knowing God

People can learn a lot. They can understand how the Earth moves, how airplanes fly, and how spaceships land on the moon. Some scientists specialize in astronomy, some in the study of nature, and others in fields like medicine and engineering.

But which of these sciences is the best and most important?

In the life of the Prophet Muhammad (s), there is a story about a man from the desert who came to him and said, "O Messenger of Allah, teach me something about the wonders of knowledge."

The Prophet of Allah (s) asked him, "Have you learned the foundation and essence of knowledge so that you can seek its wonders?" The desert man asked, "What is the foundation, O Messenger of Allah?" The Prophet (s) replied, "The foundation and essence of knowledge is knowing God."

The desert man asked, "But how can I know God?" The Prophet (a) said, "To know that God is One, and there is nothing like Him."

The desert man realized that knowing God is the basis of all knowledge. He was determined to achieve this knowledge through contemplation, thinking, and worship. Knowing God brings peace to a person and makes them a source of goodness for others. The Prophet of Allah (s) said, "Indeed, the best knowledge is knowing God."

Knowing God is the most important knowledge, and it can help us better understand the world around us. It brings peace to our hearts and guides us to do good deeds and help others.

I Lost My Wallet Inshallah!

A teacher says to her students, "Tomorrow we will learn a new lesson, Inshallah!"

And a father tells his children, "We will go on a trip this summer, Inshallah!"

What does that mean? It means that everything happens according to God's will.

Nimrod planned to burn Prophet Ibrahim (a) alive. He threw him into a roaring fire, but God intervened and turned the fire into a garden.

Even when we plan something, we say "Inshallah" because we recognize that God's plans may be different from our own.

28

Once, a man was going to the market to buy a donkey. He met a friend on the way, and his friend said, "I'm going to the market to buy a donkey."

"Say 'Inshallah'!" his friend said.

The man replied, "Why should I say 'Inshallah'? My wallet is in my pocket, and the donkeys are in the market. I'm sure I'll be able to buy one."

Later, the man saw a fine donkey and wanted to buy it. He reached into his pocket to get his wallet, but it wasn't there! He searched everywhere, but he couldn't find it.

On his way, he met another friend who asked, "Where are you going?"

The man replied, "I went to the market to buy a donkey, Inshallah, but my wallet got stolen, so now I'm returning home empty-handed, Inshallah."

✿ Prayer and Action ✿

A true believer places their trust in Allah in every aspect of life because they recognize that Allah, the Most High, is the Provider of sustenance, the Giver of life, and the Bringer of death. His power extends over all things.

In the time of the Prophet Muhammad (s), some Muslims misunderstood the concept of tawakkul, thinking it meant simply staying at home and making prayers. While it is true that a sincere believer should trust in Allah, it's also essential to work, strive, and put in effort. We can't acquire knowledge, wisdom, or wealth without dedication and hard work. Imagine someone who's lazy and expects to become a scholar or wealthy without putting in any effort.

Have you ever encountered a scholar who didn't diligently study or a person who became wealthy without any effort? The Prophet (s) once heard about some Muslims who had abandoned their work, relying solely on prayers. This deeply concerned him. He asked, "Why have you given up working and striving? Remember, Allah says, 'And whoever fears Allah, He will make for him a way out and will provide for him from where he does not expect.' We worship Allah and pray to Him, and He provides for us."

The Prophet (s) further advised them, saying, "If you abandon work, Allah won't answer your prayers. So, go out and work, for Allah has ordained a means for everything."

Which Half First?

A time long ago, there lived a righteous couple leading a peaceful and content life. One night, the husband had a dream in which an angel appeared and said, "Allah, the Most High, has ordained that your life shall be divided into two halves: One filled with prosperity and the other with challenges. You get to decide which half comes first."

The man paused and replied, "Let me consult with my wife."

His wife's choice was resolute, "In the first half, let us choose prosperity and ease. Hopefully, Allah will bestow the same upon us in the second half as well."

Their decision marked the beginning of an era of blessings. They became the proud owners of flourishing farms and lush orchards. As they neared the end of the first half of their lives, anxiety crept in. Dark clouds gathered in the sky, and they feared that their fortunes might change.

However, an angel visited them once more in a dream, delivering a message of hope, "Allah, in His divine wisdom, has decreed to bless both halves of your life. It's because you expressed gratitude for the blessings He bestowed upon you. Remember, Allah says, 'If you are grateful, I will surely increase your favor.'"

The man questioned, "Have we truly been that grateful?"

The angel assured them, saying, "Indeed, your gratitude shone through your actions. You used your blessings to obey Allah and to assist those in need. This is the most profound form of gratitude."

Allah, the Creator of all, has bestowed upon us an array of blessings. In return, it's our sacred duty to express our gratitude not merely through words but primarily through our deeds. We demonstrate our gratitude for the gift of speech by using our words honestly and abstaining from lies and gossip.

Similarly, we show our appreciation for the gift of mobility by walking towards places of goodness, such as schools and mosques, visiting loved ones and friends, and tending to the sick. In gratitude, blessings endure and flourish.

Where Were You My Angels?

Sometimes, people experience moments of anxiety, but when they turn to Allah, peace returns to their hearts, dispelling envy, selfishness, and arrogance. This shields them from the mischief of Satan. Remembering Allah goes beyond uttering phrases like "Bismillah," "Alhamdulillah," or "SubhanAllah." It involves recognizing that Allah observes us and our actions.

When we gather and engage in conversations about the mysteries of creation and the marvels of the world, it magnifies Allah's grandeur, His compassion, and His wisdom. This deepens our faith, and this, in essence, is remembering Allah.

For instance, in gatherings where the Quran is recited, supplications are made, and the lives of the righteous are discussed, there are narrations about the presence of angels. These angels attend such gatherings, offer prayers for the participants, and ascend to the heavens with forgiveness, mercy, and contentment.

In those moments, Allah questions the angels, "Where were you, My angels? The Knower of the unseen knows, but He desires to hear it from you." The angels reply, "Our Lord, we were in gatherings where You were remembered, praised, and glorified."

Allah responds, "Bear witness that I have forgiven them, and I have granted them Paradise." The angels inquire further, "Among them were people who did not remember or praise You, were there not?" Allah answers, "I have forgiven them because they sat among those who remembered Me out of generosity."

Do You Harm the One You Love?

In the annals of history, a man once sought wisdom and counsel from a respected companion of the Prophet. The companion imparted a profound piece of advice, "Never cause harm to the one you love." The man, perplexed, inquired, "Who intentionally hurts someone they love?" The companion of the Prophet responded, "You love yourself, yet you harm yourself through sinful actions."

Undoubtedly, Allah loves humanity and desires their well-being and happiness. He has prohibited actions that can harm them, such as lying, stealing, and aggression. When we engage in such transgressions, it's ourselves we harm, not Allah. It's akin to a patient who is told by a doctor not to consume a specific food—disobeying the doctor doesn't harm the doctor. Similarly, when a teacher advises students not to neglect their studies, it doesn't harm the teacher.

36

Those who truly love themselves should avoid sins because they will be held accountable for their actions.

❧ Your Knowledge and Water Droplets ❧

Now, contemplate the knowledge of Allah, the Creator of the sun, moon, stars, mountains, rivers, and the rich tapestry of life on Earth. In comparison, human knowledge appears minuscule. Even this limited knowledge is a divine gift from Allah to humanity.

Once, the Prophet Musa (a) sat with his mentor Al-Khidr (peace be upon him). They observed a bird hovering above the sea, dipping its beak into the water and then flying away, causing drops to fall into the sea. Musa asked Al-Khidr if he knew what the bird was saying.

Al-Khidr solemnly responded, "I swear by Allah, the Lord of the heavens, the earth, and the seas, that your combined knowledge, when stacked against Allah's knowledge, is no more than the drops of water that this bird has picked up with its beak when compared to the vast sea."

This story serves as a profound lesson. The bird becomes a symbol, demonstrating that our knowledge, despite our achievements, is but a fraction when measured against the boundless knowledge of Allah.

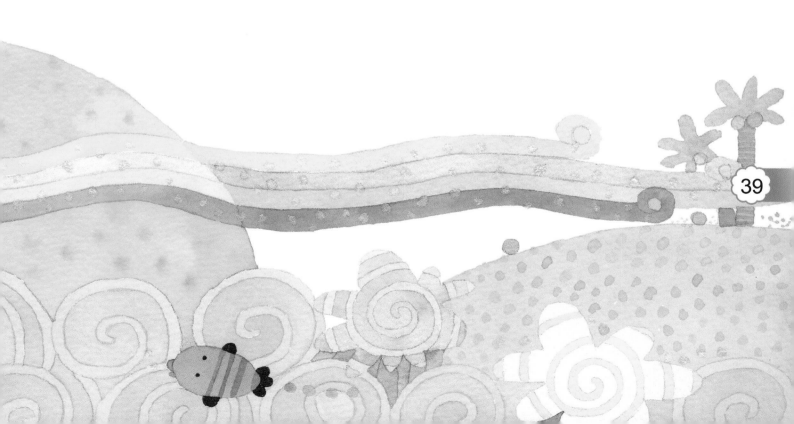

❧ The Prayer of the Ant ❧

One day, Prophet Sulaiman (a) and his followers ventured into the desert to seek divine assistance in the form of rain. Along their journey, Prophet Sulaiman noticed a remarkable sight: An ant fervently praying to God. Intrigued, he paused to hear the tiny creature's supplication. The ant, with its tiny frame, gazed skyward and pleaded, "O Lord, we are Your humble creations, beseeching You for the gift of water. Please spare us from destruction due to the transgressions of humankind."

Prophet Sulaiman's smile graced his face as he turned to his followers and declared, "You may return, for there is no need for your prayers. Allah, in response to the earnest supplication of this ant, shall send down the much-needed rain."

And indeed, it didn't take long before the heavens opened, and a deluge of rain descended, filling the streams once again.

The Signs of Allah

As we journey along a snowy path, our footprints mark our passage. In a sandy desert, tracks speak of travelers who have crossed. Tire marks on the road reveal the presence of vehicles. When feathers grace a field, we understand that a dove has soared in the sky. A wise person looks around and sees these creations and different forms of life, recognizing them as signs pointing to the Almighty Creator.

One day, the Prophet Muhammad (s) found himself in the desert, encountering a wise Bedouin. Curious, the Prophet asked, "How do you recognize your Lord?"

With profound simplicity, the Bedouin replied, "Just as camel dung signifies the presence of a camel and footprints mark a path, do not these vast deserts and the towering skies point to the knowledge and wisdom of the All-Knowing Creator?"

42

The Prophet (s) smiled, acknowledging the Bedouin's profound insight and unwavering faith.

The Believing Fisherman

In the face of poverty, some people find themselves consumed by despair and fear, unable to see a way out. They dread the prospect of not having enough food and suffering from hunger. However, there was a wise fisherman who possessed a different perspective. He held steadfast faith in Allah, the Provider of all His creations. Turning to his worried wife, he reminded her, "Who nourished us when we were in the safety of our mother's womb? Who granted us the gift of milk and a warm embrace at the moment of our birth? A true believer should never feel despair."

A believer does not feel despair ever, as he knows God created him and will look after him.

For the faithful, despair has no place, for they understand that God is their Creator, and He will watch over them.

Residing near the sea, this humble fisherman would visit the shore each morning to cast his net, content with whatever Allah's vast ocean would bestow upon him. Some of his catch would be sold in the market and the rest brought back home.

One day, despite numerous attempts, he only managed to capture a single, small fish. His wife, concerned for their future, voiced her anxieties, "If your catches continue to be so meager, we'll end up destitute, and we won't survive."

The fisherman reassured her, "Allah is the Most Merciful, and our trust in His blessings should never waver. Tomorrow, I shall return to the sea, and it is possible that Allah will provide us with more."

In the early morning, the fisherman cast his net repeatedly, only to find one small fish in his catch. His wife, with concern in her voice, asked, "You've managed to catch just one small fish?"

The fisherman replied, "We should always be grateful for the sustenance that Allah grants us. Gratitude multiplies our blessings." As he was cleaning the fish, he discovered a shining pearl inside it.

Exclaiming with joy, the fisherman declared, "This is a precious pearl! I will sell it in the market tomorrow."

With the money garnered from the pearl's sale, he returned home, proudly proclaiming to his wife, "Did I not tell you to never lose hope in Allah's boundless mercy?"

❧ The Woman Who Harms Her Neighbor ❧

Once, a group of Muslims approached the Prophet Muhammad (s) to speak in admiration of a woman within their community. One of them praised her, saying, "She dedicates her nights to prayer and worship," while another added, "She observes fasts during the day." However, a third person interjected, saying, "But she causes harm to her neighbors through her words."

Upon hearing this, the Prophet (s) responded , "There is no good in her; she is among the inhabitants of the Hellfire."

This story teaches us about how important it is to be a good person according to Allah, the Most Exalted. While praying and doing acts of worship are vital, being a good person is just as crucial. This means how you behave with your neighbors, friends, and family is just as important as your prayers.

Harming others, whether through your words or actions, goes against the idea of being a good person and a faithful believer. Allah, the Most Exalted, does not accept the prayers of those who hurt others. If you talk about people, make fun of them, or tease them, Allah won't be pleased with you. A true Muslim doesn't harm others. As the Prophet Muhammad (s) said, "A true Muslim is one from whom people find safety in their words and actions."

A Beneficial Insect

Some people might think that certain plants and insects are not useful or even ugly. But it's important to know that Allah, the Most Exalted, has created everything with a special purpose and wisdom. As time goes on, scientists discover more and more about the good things in different plants and creatures.

Once, there was a man who saw a small, black insect crawling on the ground, and he wondered why Allah made such an insect. Later, this man got a bad skin condition with painful cracks and oozing sores. He went to many doctors, but none could help him. His condition got worse, and people didn't want to be near him.

Then, a wise doctor came along and said, "I know how to cure you." The doctor went into the wilderness and collected some insects. When he came back, the man was surprised and asked, "What are you doing with those insects?"

The doctor explained, "These insects have something in their wings that can help your skin get better."

He soaked the insect wings in water and used the mixture to treat the man's sores. After a couple of days, the man's skin started to heal, and he was amazed.

He realized that Allah had a reason for making even the tiniest and plain-looking creatures. Everything Allah creates has its own wisdom and benefit.

Whoever Doesn't Thank the Creation...

In a noble Hadith, it is relayed that Allah the Almighty communicates with His servant, saying, "My dear servant, I have showered you with blessings, yet you did not express gratitude to Me."

The servant responds, "O Lord, I acknowledged Your blessings, and I offered my gratitude for the countless gifts You have bestowed upon me." The servant goes on to enumerate the blessings they've received from Allah.

However, Allah continues, "My dear servant, you failed to thank the individuals who were instrumental in facilitating the blessings I granted you. If you neglect to show them gratitude, you have, in fact, neglected to thank Me."

So, my beloved friends, it is crucial to recognize that anyone who imparts knowledge, like our dedicated teachers who invest their time and effort to educate us and bestow wisdom upon us, deserves our heartfelt appreciation and thanks. This principle extends to even the simplest acts of kindness, such as someone offering us a refreshing glass of water. Expressing gratitude is a practice that brings blessings into our lives and resonates with the teachings of Allah.

What If Allah Were to Sleep?!

In the evening, as night falls, we and all living creatures go to sleep. Birds find their way to their nests, bees return to their hives, and people head to their homes. As the sun vanishes, the cycle repeats: Birds in their nests, people in their beds, and life continues in this rhythm.

Yet, there is One who remains eternally vigilant, never slumbering or even blinking for a fraction of a second. That One is Allah, the Almighty. If Allah were to close His eyes for a moment, unimaginable chaos would ensue: planets would collide, stars would dim, springs would run dry, vision would fade, trees would wither, and life itself would come to an abrupt standstill.

A question once arose in the mind of one of the prophets: "Does Allah ever sleep?" In response, Allah directed him to hold a glass for hours on end.

As evening stretched into the night, he fought off weariness, determined to stay awake. By the time midnight approached, his eyes grew heavy, but he continued to resist the urge to sleep. However, as the dawn of a new day emerged, his eyes finally closed, and he inadvertently dropped the glass, causing it to shatter into pieces.

In that moment, the prophet comprehended the profound truth of Allah's unwavering vigilance. Allah never experiences slumber or sleep because if He were to do so, the entire world, along with all its creations, would cease to exist.

Hope is the Opposite of Despair

Hope and despair are like opposites: one casts a gloomy shadow, while the other shines radiantly with a smile. Despair can feel like a form of spiritual death, whereas hope is a vibrant force that breathes life into our existence. Even during the darkest moments, we must cling to hope, for there is always a watchful guardian—Allah, our Lord—overseeing our journey.

Allah is the One who saved the Prophet Ibrahim (a) and made the fire cool and peaceful for him. When you find yourself surrounded by adversaries who wish to cause you harm, place your trust in Allah's protective care. With hope in your heart, remember that Allah has the power to prevail over any challenge.

In the third year of the Hijra, during the Prophet Muhammad's (s) return from an expedition. The Prophet and 400 Muslims entered a valley filled with trees, and they scattered to find shade and rest. Amid the sweltering heat, the Prophet (s) sought refuge under a tree, closed his eyes, and fell into a deep slumber.

Suddenly, he awoke to the sight of a man wielding a sword, looming over him. The man demanded, "What's stopping you, Muhammad?" In response, the Prophet (s) calmly replied, "Allah is my Lord and yours." Struck by a wave of awe and kindness, the man's hand trembled, and the sword slipped from his grasp. The Prophet (s) retrieved the sword and asked the man, "What's holding you back?" The man confessed, "Your compassion and generosity." Touched by the man's sincerity, the Prophet (s) forgave him, and in return, the man pledged not to fight against the Prophet or join those who opposed him.

He returned to his people and proudly declared,
"I've come from the best of people."

A Piece of Bread Stops a Wolf!

One of the beautiful qualities of Allah, the Most Exalted, is that He deeply values the good deeds of His servants. When a person does something kind or virtuous, its positive effects can be seen not only in the Hereafter but also in this world. If you lend a helping hand to someone in need, rest assured that Allah takes note of your noble act. Apart from the rewards you'll receive on the Day of Judgment, you may also find that people in this world are more willing to assist you or shield you from potential harm.

Once upon a time, , a terrible famine had taken hold, leaving its residents struggling with extreme poverty. People's thoughts were consumed by their own desperate situations. Among them was a woman who lived with her young son. Facing the harsh reality of life, she sent her son to tend to their sheep while she ventured out in search of food.

As she wandered through the city, her search led her to discover a solitary piece of dry bread. She picked it up and began her walk back home, contemplating eating it. But then, she had a different thought. She decided to hold onto the bread and wait for her son to return from shepherding.

On her way back, her path crossed that of a destitute man who was on the brink of starvation, too weak to move. She paused and considered, "This man needs this piece of bread more than us; his hunger is far greater."

With a generous heart, she handed the bread to the hungry man and returned home with empty hands.

In the meantime, a hungry wolf, desperate for food, came dangerously close to her son, who was still shepherding. Yet, by the divine will of Allah, an angel was dispatched to shield the child from the wolf, preventing any harm. The child safely made his way back to his mother. It became clear that it was because of that selfless act of giving the piece of bread to the hungry man that Allah had protected her son and returned him safely to her.

Bismillah at Its Beginning and End

It is truly wonderful when a person begins their actions by saying, "Bismillah ar-Rahman ar-Raheem" (In the name of God, the Merciful, the Compassionate). When we utter these words, we are dedicating our actions to Allah, seeking His guidance and support.

So, whether you're getting ready for school, embarking on your homework, dressing for the day, or even when you're about to enjoy a meal, don't forget to say, "Bismillah." This simple phrase will bless your activities, make them enjoyable, and keep them pure.

If, by chance, you forget to say it and remember while you're in the middle of eating, just go ahead and say, "Bismillah."

Once, there was a companion of the Prophet (s) who was sharing a meal with him. He forgot to say, "Bismillah" before starting his meal. But just before taking the last bite, he remembered and said, "Bismillah at the beginning and end."

This thoughtful gesture brought a smile to the face of the Prophet Muhammad (s), and it resonated with other Muslims as well. It showed that what the man did was not only right but also beautiful.

The Farmer and the Potter

Long ago, there was a kind old man who had two daughters. One of his daughters was married to a farmer, and the other was married to a potter.

One day, the old man decided to visit his daughters. He went to the simple home of his daughter who was married to the farmer and asked her how she and her husband were doing. She replied, "Alhamdulillah, but I wish the rain would come down more and water our fields to help our crops grow."

The man left his daughter's home and went to visit his other daughter, the potter's wife. He asked her the same question, "How are you, my daughter? And how is your husband?" She answered, "Alhamdulillah, but I wish the weather would be sunnier to dry the pottery faster."

60

The man was a bit confused because his two daughters had completely opposite wishes. He prayed, "O Allah, You know best the needs of Your servants, and You know how to provide for them. Do what is best for them, for You are the Most Merciful and the Most Wise."

Indeed, Allah is our Merciful and Compassionate Lord, and He provides for all His creations according to what is best for them. He sends rain and sunshine at the right times to meet the needs of all living beings.

61

The Good News of Paradise

Sometimes people tend to focus on the challenges and difficulties in their lives and forget about the good things they have. This can make them complain a lot.

But there are others who see life in a more balanced way. Even when they face hard times, they remember the blessings they have and stay content and hopeful.

There's a story about the Prophet Dawud (a) who received a message from Allah to give the good news of Paradise to his neighbor. When the woman heard this, she was surprised and said, "Perhaps Allah meant to give this news to a woman with a name like mine."

The Prophet replied, "No, Allah commanded me to give you this good news." The woman was astonished and said, "I have not performed deeds deserving of such a reward."

The Prophet asked her, "What's in your heart?" She replied, "I try to be patient when things are hard, and I remember and thank Allah even in tough times."

The Prophet explained, "It's because of these qualities that Allah has chosen Paradise for you."

❦ Earning a Higher Rank ❧

It is narrated that two believers lived righteous lives, and their good deeds were similar in quantity. After their passing, they both entered Paradise. However, one of them noticed that the other held a higher rank. He asked Allah, "O Lord, my deeds that I performed are equal to his, so why did You grant him a higher rank than mine?"

Allah replied, "The one with a higher rank used to supplicate and seek this rank, but you did not."

Alongside performing good deeds, it is truly wonderful for a person to raise their hands in prayer, beseeching Allah for the elevated ranks. For actions alone may not be sufficient to achieve this.

❧ Conversations with Parents ☙

Children are the future of society, and their education is of paramount importance. Storytelling is one of the most effective tools for shaping their personalities. Children love stories, and these tales guide them toward virtuous paths with engaging narratives and beautiful imagery. Stories are a powerful means to instill values and ethics, building a strong foundation for a child's character. This collection of stories is a small contribution to the noble goal of raising the next generation, where girls grow into righteous women and noble mothers, and boys become honorable men and noble fathers.

Printed in Great Britain
by Amazon

40428042R00041